The books in this series introduce young children to the four rules of number.

This book gives over one hundred basic facts of multiplication. The lively, colourful cartoon pictures illustrate the number bonds and mathematical symbols are used under each picture. A controversy exists over whether, for example, 7 × 4 means seven lots of four or seven four times. But whichever interpretation is used (and both are considered correct) the most important thing for young children is consistency of interpretation, and the answer is in any case always the same. In this book the pictures consistently interpret the mathematical statements as 'lots of'. There are hours of fun and learning for all young children who love counting and simple arithmetic.

First edition

© LADYBIRD BOOKS LTD MCMLXXXII

Ladybird Junior Maths
MULTIPLICATION

written by
ROGER and MARY HURT

illustrated by
LYNN N GRUNDY

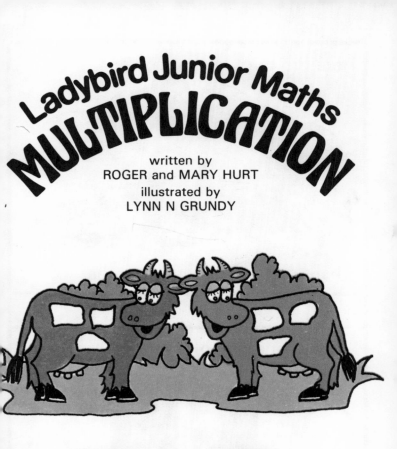

2 x 3

Ladybird Books Loughborough

Here are two *pairs* of shoes.

There are four shoes altogether.

$$2 \times 2 = 4$$

Here is one *pair* of boots.

There are two boots altogether.

$$1 \times 2 = 2$$

There isn't a pair of shoes in the box.
It is empty.

There are no shoes in the box.

$$0 \times 2 = 0$$

There are three pairs of socks
on the line.

There are six socks altogether.

$$3 \times 2 = 6$$

Here are four pairs of ears.

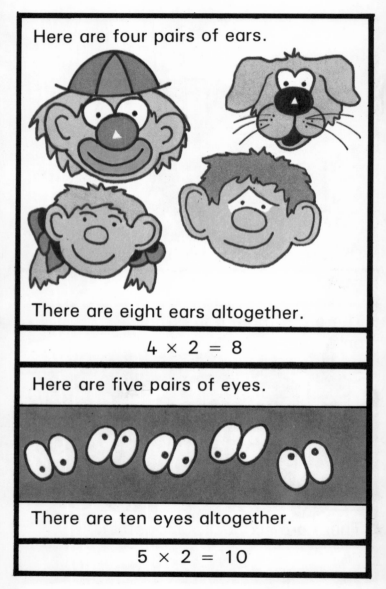

There are eight ears altogether.

$$4 \times 2 = 8$$

Here are five pairs of eyes.

There are ten eyes altogether.

$$5 \times 2 = 10$$

0	2	4	6	8	10

Count in twos.

Can you do these sums?

Count in twos.	
0	
2	
4	
6	
8	
10	

$0 \times 2 = 0$ $2 \times 0 = 0$

$1 \times 2 = 2$ $2 \times 1 = 2$

$2 \times 2 =$

$3 \times 2 =$ $2 \times 3 =$

$4 \times 2 =$ $2 \times 4 =$

$5 \times 2 =$ $2 \times 5 =$

Try to learn these facts.

0	2	4	6	8	10

Here is a tricycle.

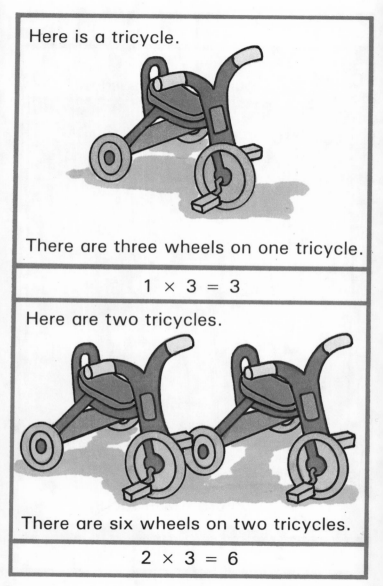

There are three wheels on one tricycle.

$$1 \times 3 = 3$$

Here are two tricycles.

There are six wheels on two tricycles.

$$2 \times 3 = 6$$

Here are three stools,
each with three legs.

There are nine legs altogether
on the stools.

$$3 \times 3 = 9$$

The stools have been put away.

Now we can see no legs at all.

$$0 \times 3 = 0$$

Here is a car.

One car has four wheels.

$$1 \times 4 = 4$$

Here are two cars.

Two cars have eight wheels.

$$2 \times 4 = 8$$

Here are three cows.

Three cows have twelve legs altogether.

$$3 \times 4 = 12$$

The cows have gone to be milked. Now we can see no legs at all.

$$0 \times 4 = 0$$

11

Which fish go into which nets?

13

Here are four skates.
Each skate has four wheels.

There are sixteen wheels
on four skates.

$$4 \times 4 = 16$$

Here are four bowls.
Each has three fish in it.

There are twelve fish
in the four bowls.

$$4 \times 3 = 12$$

What are the missing numbers?

$\bigcirc \times 2 = 4$

$2 \times \bigcirc = 8$

$\bigcirc \times 4 = 12$

$4 \times \bigcirc = 0$

$3 \times \bigcirc = 9$

$\bigcirc \times 5 = 10$

$1 \times \bigcirc = 4$

$4 \times \bigcirc = 12$

$\bigcirc \times 3 = 0$

$4 \times \bigcirc = 16$

12
11
10
9
8
7
6
5
4
3
2
1

Try to learn these facts.

Here are five dominoes.
Each has three spots.

There are fifteen spots altogether.

$$5 \times 3 = 15$$

Here are three flowers.
Each has five petals.

There are fifteen petals
on three flowers.

$$3 \times 5 = 15$$

Here are five horses.

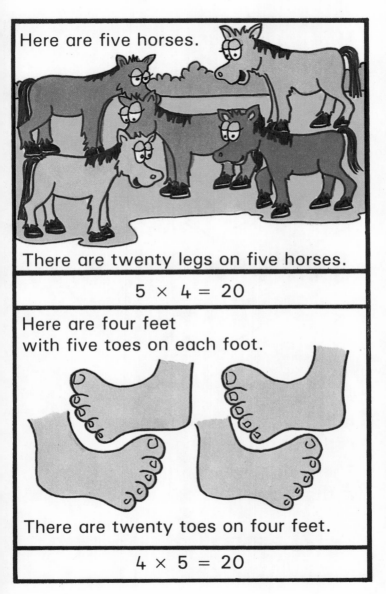

There are twenty legs on five horses.

$$5 \times 4 = 20$$

Here are four feet
with five toes on each foot.

There are twenty toes on four feet.

$$4 \times 5 = 20$$

Here is a crate of bottles.

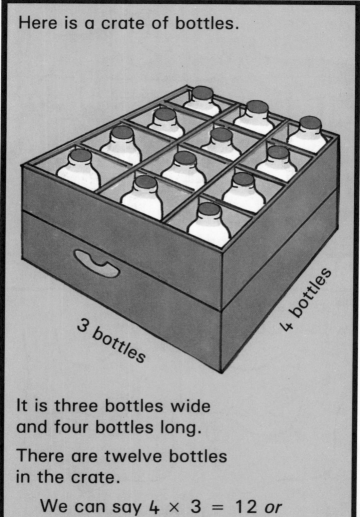

3 bottles

4 bottles

It is three bottles wide
and four bottles long.

There are twelve bottles
in the crate.

We can say $4 \times 3 = 12$ *or*
we can say $3 \times 4 = 12$

Here is a box of apples.

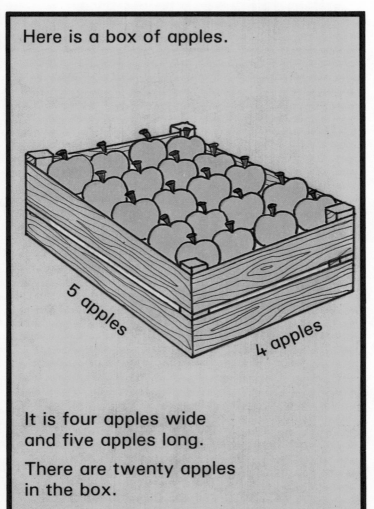

5 apples

4 apples

It is four apples wide
and five apples long.

There are twenty apples
in the box.

We can say 4 × 5 = 20 *or*
we can say 5 × 4 = 20

0	3	6	9	12	15

Count in threes.

Can you do these sums?

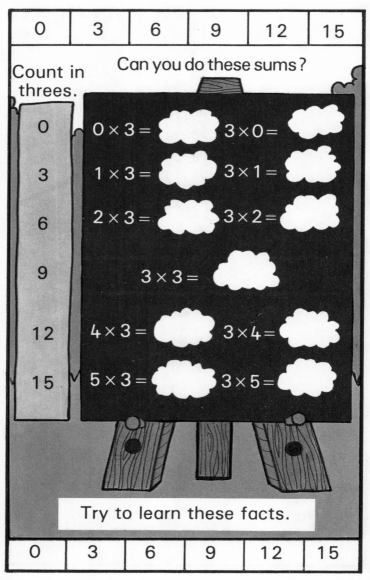

0
3
6
9
12
15

$0 \times 3 =$ $3 \times 0 =$

$1 \times 3 =$ $3 \times 1 =$

$2 \times 3 =$ $3 \times 2 =$

$3 \times 3 =$

$4 \times 3 =$ $3 \times 4 =$

$5 \times 3 =$ $3 \times 5 =$

Try to learn these facts.

0	3	6	9	12	15

Here is a glove.

There are five fingers on one glove.

$$1 \times 5 = 5$$

Here are five gloves.

There are twenty-five fingers on five gloves.

$$5 \times 5 = 25$$

| 0 | 4 | 8 | 12 | 16 | 20 |

Count in fours.

Can you do these sums?

0		
4	$0 \times 4 =$ 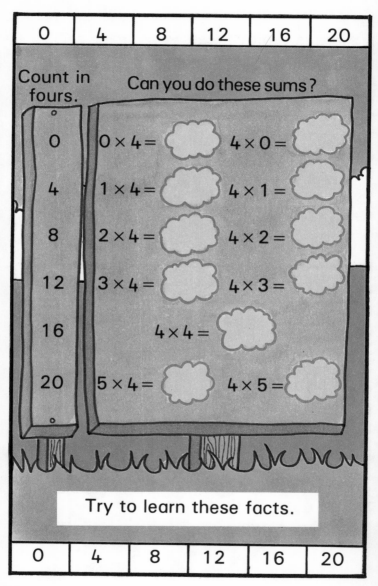	$4 \times 0 =$
8	$1 \times 4 =$	$4 \times 1 =$
12	$2 \times 4 =$	$4 \times 2 =$
16	$3 \times 4 =$	$4 \times 3 =$
20	$4 \times 4 =$	

$5 \times 4 =$ $4 \times 5 =$

Try to learn these facts.

| 0 | 4 | 8 | 12 | 16 | 20 |

Here are two boxes of eggs.
Each box has six eggs.

There are twelve eggs in two boxes.

$$2 \times 6 = 12$$

Here are three boxes of eggs.

There are eighteen eggs in three boxes.

$$3 \times 6 = 18$$

Which clowns are holding the balloons

25

| 0 | 5 | 10 | 15 | 20 | 25 |

Count in fives.

Can you do these sums?

| 0 |
| 0 |
| 5 |
| 10 |
| 15 |
| 20 |
| 25 |

0 × 5 =   5 × 0 =

1 × 5 =   5 × 1 =

2 × 5 =   5 × 2 =

3 × 5 =   5 × 3 =

4 × 5 =   5 × 4 =

5 × 5 =

Try to learn these facts.

| 0 | 5 | 10 | 15 | 20 | 25 |

If we find five nests
and each one has six eggs in it,
altogether there are thirty eggs.

$$5 \times 6 = 30$$

Here is one packet of sausages.

There are six sausages in the packet.

$$1 \times 6 = 6$$

Here are six packets of sausages.

There are thirty-six sausages
in six packets.

$$6 \times 6 = 36$$

What are the missing numbers?

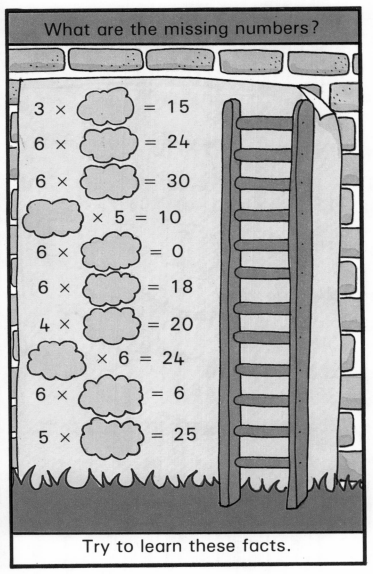

$3 \times = 15$

$6 \times = 24$

$6 \times = 30$

$ \times 5 = 10$

$6 \times = 0$

$6 \times = 18$

$4 \times = 20$

$ \times 6 = 24$

$6 \times = 6$

$5 \times = 25$

Try to learn these facts.

0	6	12	18	24	30	36

Count in sixes.

Can you do these sums?

0	$0 \times 6 =$ $6 \times 0 =$
6	$1 \times 6 =$ $6 \times 1 =$
12	$2 \times 6 =$ $6 \times 2 =$
18	$3 \times 6 =$ $6 \times 3 =$
24	$4 \times 6 =$ $6 \times 4 =$
30	$5 \times 6 =$ $6 \times 5 =$
36	$6 \times 6 =$

Try to learn these facts.

0	6	12	18	24	30	36

Here are two bunches of grapes.
There are seven grapes
in each bunch.

There are fourteen grapes
in the two bunches.

$$2 \times 7 = 14$$

Here are three bunches of grapes.

There are twenty-one grapes
in these three bunches.

$$3 \times 7 = 21$$

Here are four coats.
Each coat has seven buttons.

There are twenty-eight buttons
on the four coats.

$$4 \times 7 = 28$$

Here are seven coats, each with
seven buttons.

There are forty-nine buttons
on seven coats.

$$7 \times 7 = 49$$

Here are five flowers,
each with seven petals.

There are thirty-five petals
on five flowers.

$$5 \times 7 = 35$$

Someone has picked all the flowers,

so now we have no petals at all.

$$0 \times 7 = 0$$

Here is a ladybird.

This ladybird has seven spots.

$$1 \times 7 = 7$$

Here are six ladybirds.

These ladybirds have forty-two spots altogether.

$$6 \times 7 = 42$$

Can you do these sums?

Count in sevens		
0	$0 \times 7 =$	$7 \times 0 =$
7	$1 \times 7 =$	$7 \times 1 =$
14	$2 \times 7 =$	$7 \times 2 =$
21	$3 \times 7 =$	$7 \times 3 =$
28	$4 \times 7 =$	$7 \times 4 =$
35	$5 \times 7 =$	$7 \times 5 =$
42	$6 \times 7 =$	$7 \times 6 =$
49	$7 \times 7 =$	

Try to learn these facts.

0	7	14	21	28	35	42	49

Here is a spider.

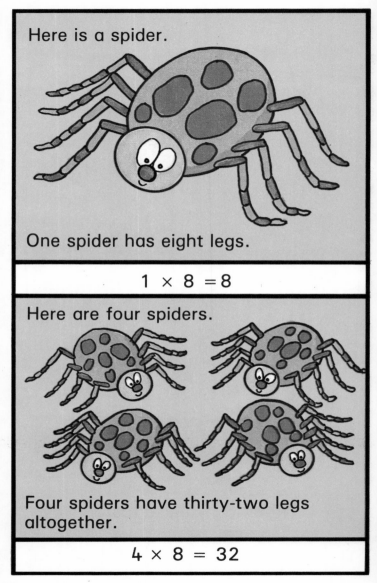

One spider has eight legs.

$$1 \times 8 = 8$$

Here are four spiders.

Four spiders have thirty-two legs altogether.

$$4 \times 8 = 32$$

Here are two octopuses.
Each one has eight legs.

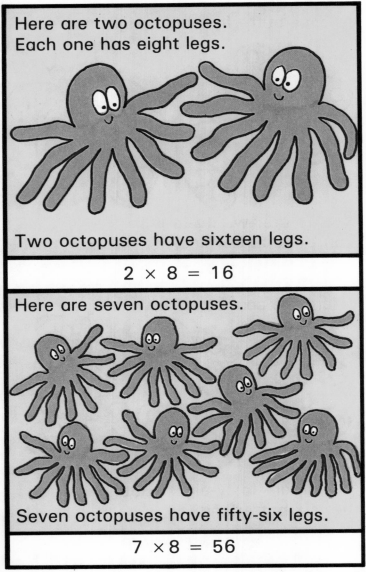

Two octopuses have sixteen legs.

$$2 \times 8 = 16$$

Here are seven octopuses.

Seven octopuses have fifty-six legs.

$$7 \times 8 = 56$$

These butterflies have eight spots.

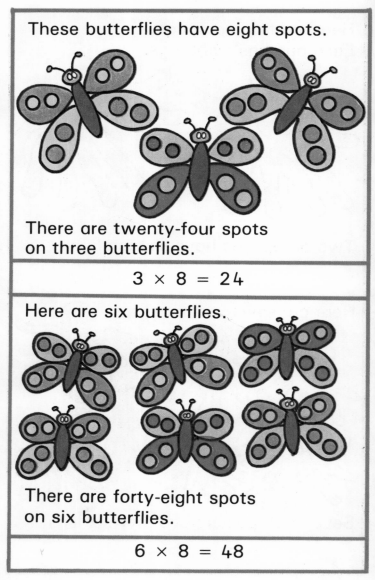

There are twenty-four spots on three butterflies.

$$3 \times 8 = 24$$

Here are six butterflies.

There are forty-eight spots on six butterflies.

$$6 \times 8 = 48$$

Count in eights.

Can you do these sums?

Count in eights	
0	
8	
16	
24	
32	
40	
48	
56	
64	

$0 \times 8 =$ $8 \times 0 =$

$1 \times 8 =$ $8 \times 1 =$

$2 \times 8 =$ $8 \times 2 =$

$3 \times 8 =$ $8 \times 3 =$

$4 \times 8 =$ $8 \times 4 =$

$5 \times 8 =$ $8 \times 5 =$

$6 \times 8 =$ $8 \times 6 =$

$7 \times 8 =$ $8 \times 7 =$

$8 \times 8 =$

Try to learn these facts.

0	8	16	24	32	40	48	56	64

Who lives in these houses?

41

These frogs have eight spots each.

Five frogs have forty spots.

$$5 \times 8 = 40$$

Here are eight frogs.

Eight frogs have sixty-four spots.

$$8 \times 8 = 64$$

What are the missing numbers?

$2 \times \boxed{} = 14$

$8 \times \boxed{} = 24$

$\boxed{} \times 7 = 42$

$1 \times \boxed{} = 8$

$\boxed{} \times 7 = 21$

$\boxed{} \times 8 = 0$

$5 \times \boxed{} = 35$

$8 \times \boxed{} = 40$

$7 \times \boxed{} = 49$

$8 \times \boxed{} = 64$

Try to learn these facts.

Here is one loaf of bread.

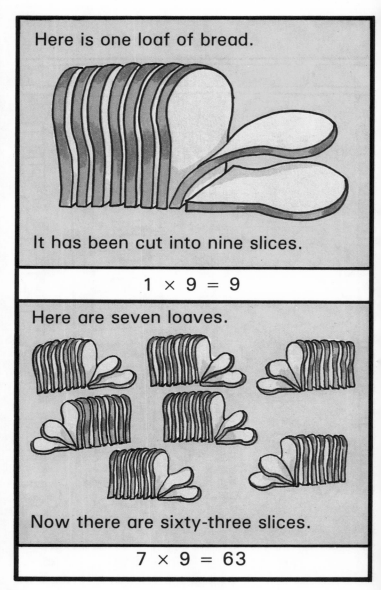

It has been cut into nine slices.

$$1 \times 9 = 9$$

Here are seven loaves.

Now there are sixty-three slices.

$$7 \times 9 = 63$$

Here are two balloon men.
Each has nine balloons.

$2 \times 9 = 18$

Now there are four men,

so there are thirty-six balloons
altogether.

$4 \times 9 = 36$

Which apples go into which baskets?

Each shield has nine crescents.

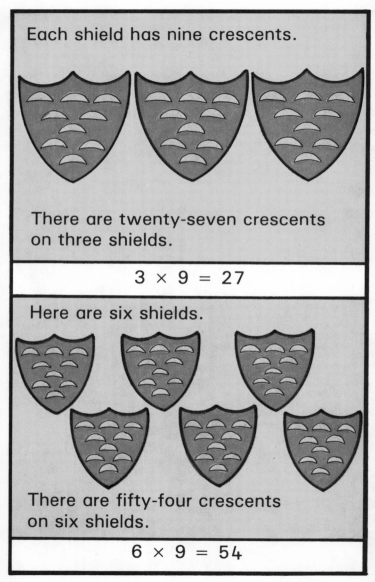

There are twenty-seven crescents on three shields.

$$3 \times 9 = 27$$

Here are six shields.

There are fifty-four crescents on six shields.

$$6 \times 9 = 54$$

Each flag has nine stars.

Five flags have forty-five stars.

$$5 \times 9 = 45$$

This castle has nine flags.

There are eighty-one stars
on nine flags.

$$9 \times 9 = 81$$

Count in nines.

Can you do these sums?

0	$0 \times 9 =$ $9 \times 0 =$
9	$1 \times 9 =$ $9 \times 1 =$
18	$2 \times 9 =$ $9 \times 2 =$
27	$3 \times 9 =$ $9 \times 3 =$
36	$4 \times 9 =$ $9 \times 4 =$
45	$5 \times 9 =$ $9 \times 5 =$
54	$6 \times 9 =$ $9 \times 6 =$
63	$7 \times 9 =$ $9 \times 7 =$
72	$8 \times 9 =$ $9 \times 8 =$
81	$9 \times 9 =$

Try to learn these facts.

0	9	18	27	36	45	54	63	72	81